Meredith Hooper is a Historian by training and a world traveller. She is
visiting Research Fellow in the History of Science at England's Royal
Institution Centre, and the winner of the Antarctica Service Medal given by
the National Science Foundation on behalf of the United States Congress,
for her service to Antarctica. Meredith's previous titles for Frances Lincoln
are *The Pebble in my Pocket*, *The Drop in my Drink*,
Tom's Rabbit – A True Story from Scott's Last Voyage, *Dogs' Night* and
Antarctic Journal – The Hidden Worlds of Antarctica's Animals.
Born in Australia, she now lives in North London.

M.P. Robertson studied Graphic Design at Kingston University.
Since 1988 he has been a freelance illustrator specialising in children's
books. Among his previous titles are *Grizelda Frizzle* with Brian Patten,
The Bed and Breakfast House with Tony Barton and
The Thwarting of Baron Bolligrew with Robert Bolt. His previous titles for
Frances Lincoln are *Seven Ways to Catch the Moon* and *The Egg*,
both of which he wrote and illustrated. M.P. Robertson lives in
Wiltshire, with his partner the illustrator Sophy Williams,
and their two young children.

**Boat Journey in James Caird,
24 Apr – 10 May 1916**

**ELEPHANT
ISLAND**

SOUTHERN OCEAN

*Boats launched,
9 Apr 1916*

*The men camp on
drifting ice floes,
27 Oct 1915 –
9 Apr 1916*

Endurance *sinks,
21 Nov 1915*

Endurance *crushed.
Crew abandons ship,
27 Oct 1915*

WEDDELL SEA

ANTARCTIC PENINSULA

Pack Ice

Ice Shelf

Endurance *trapped
in pack ice,
18 Jan 1915*

Arrival at Stromness Whaling Station, 20 May 1916

SOUTH GEORGIA

Departure from Grytviken Whaling Station, 5 Dec 1914

SOUTH SANDWICH ISLANDS

| 0 miles | 125 | 250 | 375 | 500 |

SOUTH AMERICA

ANTARCTICA

TASMANIA

NEW ZEALAND

AUSTRALIA

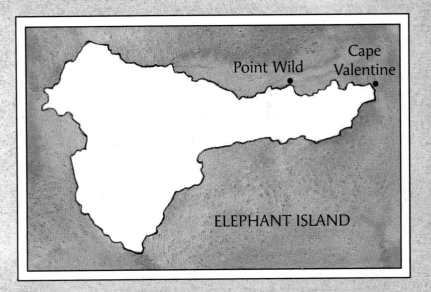

Point Wild

Cape Valentine

ELEPHANT ISLAND

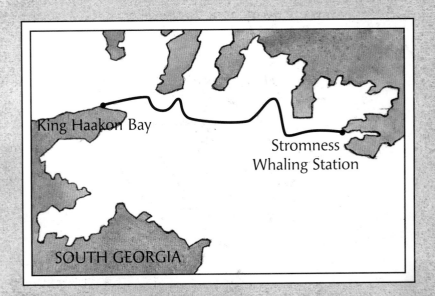

King Haakon Bay

Stromness Whaling Station

SOUTH GEORGIA

To the ship's company of HMS Endurance – M.H.
To Gammack, Jupp, Jones, Nighy and Knox. For tennis and Thursday nights – M.P.R.

ACKNOWLEDGEMENTS

The Author would like to thank the Commanding Officer of HMS *Endurance* for giving her the opportunity to land on Elephant Island; the Captain of R/V *Laurence M. Gould* for enabling her to track the Island's coast by sea; and the United States National Science Foundation for taking her to Antarctica on their Artists & Writers Program.

Frances Lincoln would like to thank Captain Tim Barton RN, William Mills of the Scott Polar Research Institute and Dr Jan Piggott of Dulwich College for their help.

Text copyright © Meredith Hooper 2000
Illustrations copyright © M.P. Robertson 2000
Photographs on pp28-29 by Frank Hurley, with the
kind permission of the Royal Geographical Society, London

First published in Great Britain in 2000 by
Frances Lincoln Limited,4 Torriano Mews,
Torriano Avenue, London NW5 2RZ

British Library Cataloguing in Publication Data available on request

ISBN 0-7112-1713-0 hardback
ISBN 0-7112-1744-0 paperback

Printed in Hong Kong

1 3 5 7 9 8 6 4 2

ICE TRAP!

Shackleton's Incredible Expedition

MEREDITH HOOPER • M.P. ROBERTSON

FRANCES LINCOLN

"Stowaway! Stowaway!" The locker lid crashed back and Percy Blackborrow staggered out into the bitter air. For three days he'd crouched inside the dark locker under piles of clothes while the ship pitched through the ocean. Now he felt so seasick and hungry he didn't mind being discovered.

Suddenly Sir Ernest Shackleton was standing above him, roaring his anger.

"Do you know," bellowed Shackleton, "that on these expeditions we often get very hungry, and if there is a stowaway available he is the first to be eaten?"

Percy looked up. Shackleton was a heavy, powerfully-built man. "They'd get a lot more meat off you, sir!" he said.

Shackleton turned away to hide a grin. "Off to the cook for some food," he said. "Then we'll sign you on."

So nineteen-year-old Percy Blackborrow became the youngest member of Sir Ernest Shackleton's great Imperial Trans-Antarctic Expedition. Shackleton wanted to be the first to walk across the Antarctic continent, 1,800 miles from coast to coast. No one even knew the actual shape of this awesome, ice-covered land at the bottom of the world.

But before that, Shackleton had to get his wooden ship *Endurance* through the thickest, most dangerous pack ice in Antarctica.

Endurance entered the pack ice in high summer. The floes glittered like endless ice-white fields. Week after week the ship worked south, weaving and charging through the vast jigsaw of ice, finding open patches of indigo blue sea, dodging icebergs.

Shackleton wanted to get his men ashore as far south as possible, with all their gear and their excited sledging dogs. One more day's good sailing should do it. Pieces of ice crowded around the ship, so they stopped and waited. Pack ice is always on the move, shoving together, then loosening up, as the pieces drift and shift.

But now a gale began, packing the ice tighter.

Before anyone realised what was happening, the ice had hardened around *Endurance* like cement. She was stuck fast, glued into a vast thick floe. "Frozen in," said the Captain, Frank Worsley, "like a nut in a chocolate bar."

The ice drifted, carrying *Endurance* with it. The men could see land in the distance, but they were powerless to go where they wanted. *Endurance* began to drift away from the coast they had striven so hard to reach, back towards the north. The temperature plummeted. Summer was nearly over. A new journey had begun. Unplanned. Unwanted.

Winter came with fearful cold and dreadful darkness. The sun did not rise for 79 days. The dogs curled up out on the floe in 'dogloos' made of iceblocks. Inside the warm ship the men argued about what was happening in the rest of the world, and when they would break free from their lonely prison. They played cards, and practical jokes, and were bored.

Outside, the silence was eerie. But every now and then ominous moans and clatters in the distance told of huge ice floes grinding together, neither giving way, massive blocks of rock-hard ice heaving up in jumbled piles.

One night when the wind howled in the rigging, Shackleton talked to Frank Worsley. "The ship can't live in this," he said. "It's only a matter of time." He paced restlessly in his tiny cabin. "What the ice gets, the ice keeps."

Worsley couldn't bring himself to believe it. In any case they said nothing to the others. Cheerfulness, optimism – that's what mattered.

The ice would release its grip. *Endurance* would escape.

Late in the winter the floe trapping *Endurance* broke during a storm. All around, the ice heaped up in confused ridges like giant wrinkled skin. The pieces ground together again, squeezing the ship. *Endurance* was heaved high, thrown on one side, then righted herself. But bit by bit her strong thick timbers buckled, bent, then splintered and cracked under the terrible, roaring pressure. Day after day the ship groaned like a living thing. The dogs howled. The men watched, helpless.

The end came suddenly one afternoon. Giant fingers of ice forced themselves through the ship's sides. Freezing black water poured into the hold and cabins. Like some terrible animal the ice fingers held the ship, stopping her sinking.

The men tumbled out onto the floe. Their home had gone. Watching their ship die was shocking.

Shackleton looked around at his men's tired anxious faces. Their safety was all that mattered now. They must believe that they would survive.

"Ship and stores have gone," said Shackleton. "So now we'll go home."

The nearest land was hundreds of miles across the pack ice. No one lived there, or ever had. But Shackleton ordered everyone to start marching, dragging the heavy lifeboats across the tortuous ice surface.

The first day they managed less than a mile. The second and third days they travelled three-quarters of a mile. It was no use. They would have to set up camp.

A thick flat floe was chosen for a camp site. Men walked back to the twisted broken ship and salvaged what they could.

Life on the floe wasn't bad. The cook served breakfast at 8 o'clock and they sat in their tents and ate fried seal, or tinned fish, or porridge, with lumps of baked dough and tea. For supper they had penguin stew and cocoa. Spring had come so there were plenty of seals and penguins to eat.

Late one afternoon *Endurance* suddenly upended and sank beneath the ice. They felt very lonely now. The floe they were camping on seemed solid but it was really just a giant floating raft, drifting ever northwards. Underneath their feet lay 12,000 feet of deep dark ocean.

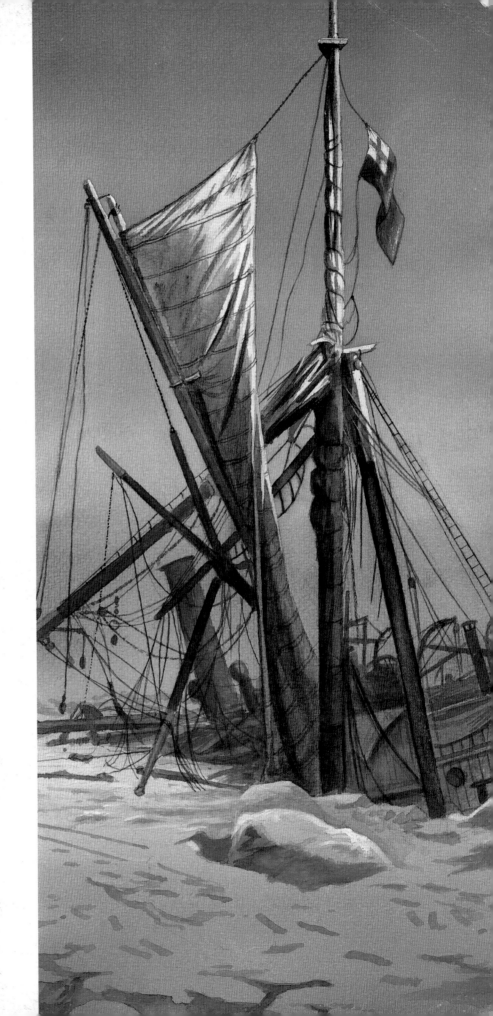

Shackleton paced the floe as it drifted in zigzags north. Summer was almost over. The last of the dogs were shot – there wasn't enough food for them. The men sat in their ragged dirty clothes, fidgety, anxious, watching Shackleton. Their lives depended on his decisions.

At the northern edge of the pack ice the ocean swell bashed at the ice floes, breaking them up. Their floe was drifting ever closer to this treacherous border between ice and open ocean. They would have to take to the lifeboats.

Their floe heaved and tilted in the ocean swell. Bits broke off. Shackleton ordered everyone to sleep fully clothed, with boots on, ready to be out of the tents in 30 seconds. Only absolute necessities could be taken in the boats. But each man still kept hidden his own carefully hoarded treasures – a photograph, or a Bible, or a tube of toothpaste.

The floe split through the camp. It split again. All around them the ice crashed and lurched. Shackleton watched, waiting for a lead – a gap of clear water. Suddenly it came. The boats were launched, the men scrambled in and bent to the oars.

They had been trapped in the ice prison for 15 months. But the ocean was a much more dangerous, frightening enemy. Their small boats could easily be crushed between jolting grinding floes; out in the ocean, overloaded and open, they could easily be swamped.

By the sixth day of their voyage they were desperate with lack of sleep and hunger. They could hardly speak for thirst, their skin erupted with sea-water boils, they were weak with diarrhoea. Spray shipped from heavy seas froze as it fell on their bitterly cold, frost-bitten, soaking bodies. Shackleton feared that some of his men would not survive.

Ahead they could see the high mountains and white glaciers of Elephant Island, rising bleak and grand out of the wild ocean. Late in the afternoon a gale blew up, with a dangerous lumpy sea. They feared being swept in the snow storms and shrieking wind past the island, and beyond all hope.

But at dawn the land lay straight ahead. A narrow beach was glimpsed, backed by black cliffs. Riding the surf they managed to bring all three boats ashore between jagged rocks.

It was land, solid, real, dry land at last. Men staggered along the grey sand, half mad with relief, laughing, crying. Then they slept, and the sharp stones sticking into their shoulders just made them happier because stones meant the land, not the terrible sea, or the heaving ice.

But they were not saved. The beach was a death-trap. High tides could sweep to the base of the cliffs, and the cliffs were too steep to climb. Shackleton forced the men back into the boats.

No one wanted to face the ocean again, but along the coast a safer place to camp had been found. It was only a low spit of sand and boulders with a glacier at one end and mess from nesting penguins. They pitched their worn-out tents. In the night a roaring gale ripped a tent and snow covered the sleeping bags. The men were too weary to care.

Elephant Island was uninhabited. Harsh mountains loomed through the swirling cloud. Thick glaciers tumbled to the coast. Some of the men despaired. To go through so much, for this. No one would ever find them here.

The gale blew precious cooking pots into the sea, and tossed lumps of ice on to their tattered gear. Shackleton gathered everyone and, shouting against the roar of the wind, told them his final plan. He would fetch help. They would be rescued. With five chosen men he would take the strongest boat and sail to the island of South Georgia where there were whaling stations, men and ships.

South Georgia lay 800 miles away across the world's stormiest wildest ocean. Winter was beginning. The *James Caird* was only 23 feet long, an open wooden lifeboat. The risk was terrible, unbelievable.

Shackleton shook hands with each of his men. Standing forlornly on the beach in their patched thin clothes, they cheered bravely. If anyone could get through, it would be the Boss.

Next morning the pack ice closed in.

Day after day the *James Caird* tumbled and jerked in gale-swept seas. The men could only crawl in the gloomy, sodden little living space below the scrap of canvas deck. Their sleeping bags and clothes were soaked. Once an enormous freak wave came from nowhere and swamped the boat. They bailed the freezing water for their lives and slowly the shuddering, sopping, lurching little craft lifted and became buoyant again. Then their fresh water ran out and they suffered agonies of thirst.

They feared that they would miss the island in the vast ocean and sail on to their deaths. Almost miraculously, on the 15th day, they saw black cliffs looming ahead and shouted for joy. Then a terrible hurricane began roaring in, battering the *James Caird*, almost wrecking them on the very coast they had sailed so far to reach. Desperately bailing, inching back from treacherous rocks in a seething tormented sea, they pretended to each other that they'd get through. But they knew they were looking Death square in the eye.

Tired beyond belief they managed on the 17th day to land in a small cove. They were on the wrong side of the island. No one lived there. But they were safe.

The last journey was over land. They had to walk across the high mountain passes, the glaciers and snow fields of South Georgia. A journey that had never been made before.

Shackleton, Frank Worsley and big Tom Crean set off in the moonlight, leaving their three exhausted companions camping under the overturned *James Caird*. They carried a length of rope, the carpenter's axe, a cooker and matches, a watch and a compass, and enough food for six meals in three socks.

As darkness fell at the end of the first day, they found themselves high on a mountain pass, on the edge of a sharp razor-back ridge of ice. Fog crept up towards them, drifting around their legs. Gingerly, Shackleton climbed over the ridge and began cutting footholds in the ice down the other side. But they weren't descending fast enough. With night coming on, they would freeze at this altitude.

Below, somewhere in the darkness, the ice slope either eased, or steepened into a precipice. They took the risk. Coiling the rope under their bottoms they made themselves into a human toboggan and pushed off, terrifyingly, hair-raisingly fast. At first silent with fear, then yelling with excitement, they hurtled down the slope and fell into a bank of snow. They'd descended 1,500 feet in three minutes. Their trousers were in tatters. But they had survived.

At last, 36 hours after setting off, they found themselves walking towards the whaling station. Two children saw them.

"Where is the Manager's house?" asked Shackleton. The children stared one horrified stare at the three filthy men with matted hair and beards, and fled.

Shackleton, Worsley and Crean had been wearing the same torn greasy clothes for six months. Their bloodshot eyes blinked wearily in scarred, blackened faces. But they had done what they set out to do.

On Elephant Island the 22 men left behind built a hut under the remaining boats, with walls made of tent canvas and boulders. There was no room to stand upright. It was their bedroom, bathroom, sitting-room, hospital, all in one dark, filthy, smelly, smoky, greasy space. Some of the men were sick, some injured. The frost-bitten toes on Percy Blackborrow's left foot had to be amputated.

The men huddled around the fire, taking turns so everyone had a chance to sit near the heat. The evening meal was over by five. Then in the gloom they climbed into their wet sleeping bags and sang all the songs they knew, to the twanging sound of a banjo. Every night someone read a recipe out of a little cookbook, and they imagined wonderful meals. Then they lay listening to the beat of the surf, the ice cracking on the glacier, the winter storms hurling stones through the air. The months went by.

Food began to run out. But whenever the sea was clear of ice their leader Frank Wild said, "Roll up your sleeping bags, boys. The Boss may come today."

Week after week, Shackleton tried to find a way to rescue his men on Elephant Island. The whalers on South Georgia lent a ship but it couldn't get through the pack ice. Shackleton managed to borrow another ship, and another, but each time the ice won.

In a last desperate attempt, the Chilean Navy lent a little iron steamer, the *Yelcho*. Shackleton promised not to let it touch the ice. "We shall either die, or return with the shipwrecked men," wrote the Chilean commander to his father.

And this time the weather stayed fine, the pack ice moved away. The men on Elephant Island were sitting down to a stew of old seal bones when they heard a yell of "Ship!" from someone outside. The precious soup was kicked over. They tumbled out of the hut, and rushed into the rescue boat. Shackleton allowed no delay. He feared that the pack ice would blow back in, any moment. Just under an hour from arriving at the camp on the sand spit, the *Yelcho* headed out to sea again.

"I have done it," said Shackleton. "At last. Not a life lost."

It is one of the greatest stories of rescue and survival ever.

8 AUGUST Shackleton and his men sail from England on their expedition to Antarctica, just as the First World War begins.

5 DECEMBER *Endurance* leaves the ice-covered island of South Georgia, and reaches the edge of the Antarctic pack ice, in the Weddell Sea, three days later.

18 JANUARY *Endurance* is frozen in the pack ice at the southern edge of the Weddell Sea.

27 OCTOBER *Endurance* is crushed by the ice, after drifting north for 9 months. Shackleton and his men abandon ship and begin living on the pack ice.

1914

1915

9 APRIL The floe they are camping on reaches the edge of the pack ice. The shipwrecked men finally take to their three lifeboats.

15 APRIL They land at Cape Valentine, Elephant Island, 160 miles north of the Antarctic Peninsula. Two days later they travel along the coast to Point Wild, where they set up camp.

24 APRIL Shackleton leaves with five men in the 23-foot *James Caird*, to get help at South Georgia, 800 miles to the east.

10 MAY The *James Caird* sails across the ocean, and reaches South Georgia. The exhausted men come ashore at King Haakon Bay.

1916 continued

THE *AURORA* – SHACKLETON'S SECOND SHIP

Shackleton's plans to walk 1,800 miles across Antarctica included a second ship, the *Aurora*, landing a party of men at Ross Island on the opposite side of the continent. These men had orders to walk part way to the South Pole, leaving supplies for Shackleton's party slogging across from the Weddell Sea. The men of the *Aurora* struggled in dreadful conditions to leave supplies, not knowing that Shackleton had never even landed on the continent. Three men died. The survivors were not rescued until January 1917.

TRANS-ANTARCTIC EXPEDITION

30 OCTOBER – 1 NOVEMBER
A march begins across the pack ice towards the distant land. The 28 men manage less than two miles, then set up Ocean Camp on the drifting ice.

21 NOVEMBER
Endurance sinks.

23-29 DECEMBER
The pack ice drifts slowly north. They try walking to land again, leaving many things behind, but they fail. They set up Patience Camp on a new floe.

23 MARCH
They see land for the first time on the 139th day of drifting since *Endurance* sank, but it is impossible to reach.

1916

19-20 MAY
Shackleton, Worsley and Crean walk across South Georgia, 40 miles in 36 hours, to the Norwegian whaling station at Stromness.

23 MAY
The men marooned at Elephant Island wait to be rescued. Shackleton leaves South Georgia on a first attempt, but cannot get through the ice.

25 AUGUST
Shackleton leaves Punta Arenas, Chile in the *Yelcho* on his fourth attempt to reach Elephant Island.

30 AUGUST
All the men are rescued from Elephant Island.

SIR ERNEST SHACKLETON

Ernest Shackleton was born in Ireland on 15 February 1874, moving to England when he was 10. In 1901 he went to Antarctica on an expedition commanded by Robert Scott. Scott chose him to join his small party of three which walked some distance towards the South Pole. Shackleton almost reached the South Pole on his own expedition in 1907-9. Then came the Imperial Trans-Antarctic Expedition, 1914-1917. Shackleton died suddenly in South Georgia on 5 January 1922, aged 47, on his way to the Antarctic again.

Boat Journey in James Caird,
24 Apr – 10 May 1916

**ELEPHANT
ISLAND**

SOUTHERN OCEAN

Boats launched,
9 Apr 1916

The men camp on
drifting ice floes,
27 Oct 1915 –
9 Apr 1916

Endurance *sinks,*
21 Nov 1915

Endurance *crushed.*
Crew abandons ship,
27 Oct 1915

WEDDELL SEA

ANTARCTIC PENINSULA

Pack Ice

Ice Shelf

Endurance *trapped*
in pack ice,
18 Jan 1915

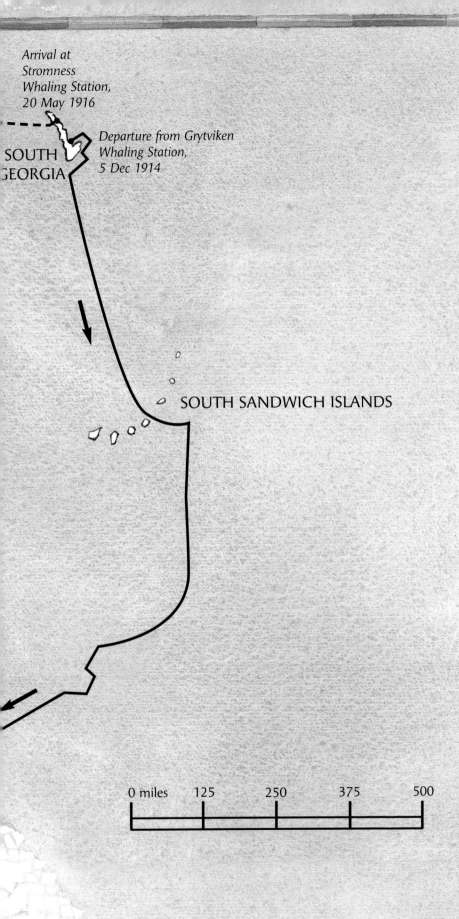

Arrival at Stromness Whaling Station, 20 May 1916

SOUTH GEORGIA

Departure from Grytviken Whaling Station, 5 Dec 1914

SOUTH SANDWICH ISLANDS

| 0 miles | 125 | 250 | 375 | 500 |

SOUTH AMERICA

ANTARCTICA

TASMANIA

NEW ZEALAND   AUSTRALIA

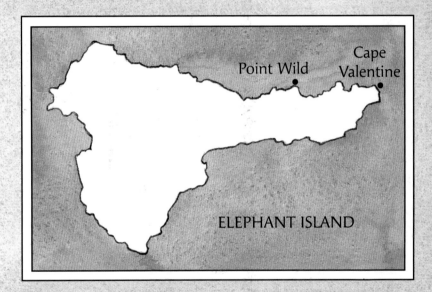

Point Wild   Cape Valentine

ELEPHANT ISLAND

King Haakon Bay

Stromness Whaling Station

SOUTH GEORGIA

MORE PICTURE BOOKS IN PAPERBACK BY MEREDITH HOOPER

TOM'S RABBIT
Illustrated by Bert Kitchen

Based on diaries by men on Scott's second Antarctic expedition,
this is the heart-warming story of sailor Tom Crean and his pet rabbit.
ISBN 0-7112-1184-1 £5.99

Suitable for National Curriculum English – Reading, Key Stage 1; History, Key Stage 1; Geography, Key Stage 1
Scottish Guidelines English Language – Reading, Levels A and B; Environmental Studies, Levels A and B

THE PEBBLE IN MY POCKET
Illustrated by Chris Coady

The story of a pebble over 480 million years,
in an awe-inspiring look at the Earth's dramatic history.
ISBN 0-7112-1076-4 £5.99

Suitable for National Curriculum English – Reading, Key Stages 2 and 3; Science, Key Stages 2 and 3
Scottish Guidelines English Language – Reading, Level D; Environmental Studies - Level D

DOGS' NIGHT
Illustrated by Allan Curless

Once a year, the dogs in the paintings in the National Gallery
come to life and spend the evening playing and exploring.
But one year, some of the dogs climb back into the wrong paintings...
A hilarious introduction to great art, for young children.
ISBN 0-7112-1461-1 £5.99

Suitable for National Curriculum English – Reading, Key Stage 1; Art, Key Stage 1
Scottish Guidelines English Language – Reading, Levels A and B; Art and Design, Level B

Frances Lincoln titles are available from all good bookshops.
Prices are correct at time of publication, but may be subject to change.